Illustrated by
Yevheniia Lisovaya

Written by
Courtney North

Have you ever looked up at the **sky at night**?
Have you ever seen a **shooting star**?

What if it wasn't a shooting star.
What if it was a **UFO**?

And what if it wasn't just any old UFO...

What if it was a UFO belonging to
Beenz, the coolest alien in the galaxy.

This is Beenz, and this is his pet, Peace.

Beenz and Peace live **far away** on the other side of our **Solar System**.

Their home is a planet called **Saturn**.
It's the big yellow one, between Jupiter and Uranus.

That's it, you've found it!

Beenz and Peace live very happily on Saturn
nowadays, but it wasn't always that way.

Oh no, there was a time when Beenz was miserable.
Very miserable.

In fact, he was the most miserable alien in the galaxy.

Would you like to know the story of how Beenz stopped being miserable, and learned to find his happy place?

It all started a long time ago as Beenz was taking Peace for his morning walk one day.

"Where shall we go today, Peace?" said Beenz.
"**Wiff,**" barked Peace (that's how alien dogs bark).

"An excellent idea, Peace,"
said Beenz, patting his pet.
"Off to the park it is."

So, Beenz and Peace set off for a walk to the park.
They hadn't even got to the end of the road when a
stranger stopped them.

"Good morning. And **where are you from?**" asked the stranger.

"Good morning," replied Beenz. "**I'm from over there**," he said. And he pointed back down the road to his house.

"Oh, sorry," said the stranger, "I thought that you were from another planet."

"Why did you think that?" asked Beenz.

"Why, because **you look so different**, that's why," said the stranger.

Beenz looked at the stranger, *then he looked at himself.*

"**We don't look that different,**" he said. "Look, we both have eyes and arms and legs."

"But look at your big tooth! No one else on Saturn has a big tooth like that."
And with that, the stranger walked off.

Beenz shook his head and said to Peace, "Well, I don't know what he's talking about. Everyone looks a bit the same and a bit different, don't they? Why, even you and I look a bit the same and a bit different, don't we, Peace?"

So, Beenz and Peace walked on through the park gate. They hadn't even got to the playground when two **more strangers stopped them**.

"Hello! Lovely day. **Are you visiting here**?" asked the second stranger.

"No," said Beenz. He was starting to get a bit annoyed. "I live over there," he said.

"Do you?" said the third stranger. "**That's strange, because you don't look like us at all**."

"Don't I?" said Beenz. "But we all have feet and hands and faces."

"But just look at your silly hat!" said the second stranger.

Beenz took his hat off and looked at it. 'What's wrong with my hat,' he thought?

The strangers walked on, and so did Beenz and Peace. Peace yapped and wiffed and begged to play ball, but for some reason, Beenz didn't feel like playing anymore.

In the playground, they met another stranger who thought that **Beenz' clothes were strange**. And by the woods, they met another who thought that **Beenz talked funny**.

"It's because of my tooth," explained Beenz.

"Well, it's not normal, whatever the reason," said the stranger.

Beenz looked around at all the other aliens in the park. Until now, he'd thought that everyone looked a bit the same and a bit different. But now, he wondered if perhaps all the strangers were right. Did everyone else look the same? Was it just Beenz who was different?

"Wiff!" barked Peace.
"And you're different too, Peace!"
"If I don't belong here on Saturn," said Beenz,
"then where do I belong?"
"Wiff, wiff, wiff!" barked Peace.
"You're a genius, Peace! That's exactly what we'll do!" cried Beenz.

And they rushed home at once and packed up the UFO.

Off they set, out into the dark night of space.
First stop: Uranus.

"Perhaps I will fit in on Uranus," said Beenz.
But Uranus was cold, and Uranus was empty.
"There's no one here at all!" said Beenz.
"We couldn't fit in even if we wanted to!"

So off they set again. Next stop: Mercury.

"This is more like it!" said Beenz.
"Not so cold, and not so empty."

There were aliens on Mercury, but they didn't speak Beenz' language, and he didn't speak theirs.

"They seem nice, but I wish I understood what they were saying," sighed Beenz. "I don't think I'm from here either."

So off they set again. Final stop: Jupiter.

This is more like it!" said Beenz.
Jupiter's temperature was just like Saturn's.
And Jupiter was colorful, and Jupiter was full of friendly aliens of all shapes and sizes.

The aliens welcomed Beenz and admired his clothes and hat. They didn't think that he looked strange; they thought that he looked funky.

For the first time in his life, Beenz felt at home.

"This must be where I'm from," he told Peace.
"Everyone's different here, so we're all the same."

Beenz and Peace stayed on Jupiter for many days and nights. They played racing games and hide-and-seek. They sang and danced and ate delicious food.

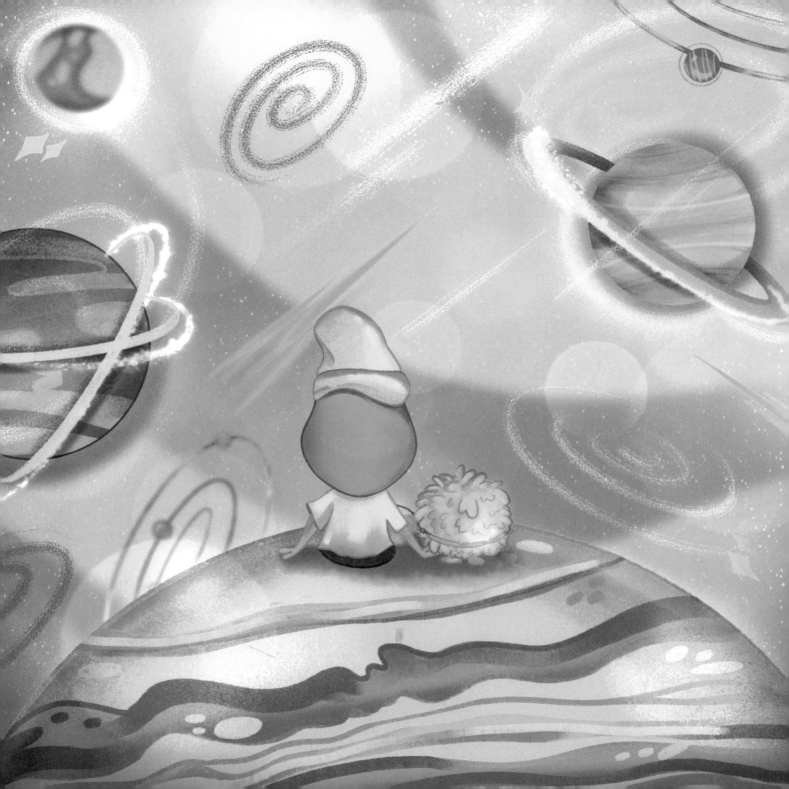

But after a while, Beenz began to get a strange feeling in his tummy.

"Wiff!" said Peace.
"You're right, Peace!" said Beenz. "**Maybe I miss home.**"

Beenz looked up at the starry sky towards Saturn. "Jupiter's fun, and the people are friendly, but it's not where I'm from. I'm from Saturn."

Suddenly, he had an idea!

"It's not me who looks too different, everyone else just looks the same! We're not meant to fit in! We're meant to stand out! Come on, Peace!"

And they jumped back into their UFO towards home.

Beenz landed back on Saturn and parked his UFO in front of the Town Hall.

"Fellow citizens of Saturn. You may think that I do not belong here. You may think that I am too different. But I have traveled our Solar System, and I have learned something. That being different is not a weakness."

The crowd gasped.

"Being different is a strength.
We are all different.
And that is why we all belong here!"

Many aliens in the crowd shook their heads.
But one young alien began to clap, followed by
another, and then another. Until soon, **the whole
crowd was clapping and cheering for Beenz**.

The next morning when he took Peace to the park, Beenz was the one to stop and talk to a stranger.

"Cool hat," said Beenz.

"Thank you, Beenz," said the stranger.
"I've had this hat for years. I never dared to wear it before because I thought that it was too different. **Now, thanks to you, I feel confident to be myself.**"

When Beenz got to the playground, he stopped someone with funky sneakers.

"Nice sneakers," said Beenz.
"Thanks, Beenz! **You're my hero.** I feel much more like myself in these funky sneakers now!"

As Beenz and Peace walked around the park, they noticed that more and more aliens were dressed in different and funky clothes.

Everyone looked
different.

And everyone
looked happier.

"See, Peace, we really do belong here
on Saturn after all.
No one fits in, so everyone belongs."

"Wiff!" agreed Peace.

**And that's the story of how
Beenz found his happy place: home.**

ABOUT THE AUTHOR

Leading wordsmith extraordinaire and creative adventurer, Courtney North is a highly passionate author whose sole mission is to inspire children to surface their genuine selves. Based in Utah, Courtney has spent 10 years of her career in Education, is an empowerment-driven entrepreneur at Don't Fit In, a proud mom to a 6-year-old son, and a lifelong learner who demonstrates that it is possible to unravel barriers and unearth the confidence necessary to live a prospering, authentic life.

Growing up, Courtney was never one to fit inside the societal mold. Though this hindered her early on, she used it as stepping stones to discover her true self and now proudly showcases it to the world. Though it did take a lot of unlearning, learning, healing, and motivation from her son to keep advancing, it was a valuable journey worth taking on, and this is the same level of dedication and perseverance she instilled into her characters. Overall, she has a true ardency for her work and demonstrates that by delivering compelling, authentic storylines that support childhood development and helps them surface new perspectives to unlock their true potential.

As a family-oriented, fun-loving author of the new children's book called "Beenz and Peace Find Their Happy Place," nothing makes Courtney happier than being able to deliver moving publications that foster positive change within young minds. She enjoys being able to create captivating, unpredictable plots with encouraging characters that leave lasting impressions, truly pulling her little readers in from cover to cover.

Made in the USA
Columbia, SC
24 October 2021

BEENZ & PEACE
& PEACE
FIND THEIR
HAPPY PLACE

Courtney North

Written by
Courtney North

This book is dedicated to:

Everyone I love,
Especially, my little dude, Sawyer, there is no one like YOU
here on this earth and you are so special to me.

This book is inspired by all those who dare to be different.

DON'T SIT STILL. DON'T FIT IN.

Published in association with Bear With Us Productions

ISBN: 979-8-746-08940-3